ROSTER REBOUND

BY JAKE MADDOX

Text by Natasha Deen
Illustrated by Maria Lia Malandrino

STONE ARCH BOOKS
a capstone imprint

Published by Stone Arch Books, an imprint of Capstone
1710 Roe Crest Drive, North Mankato, Minnesota 56003
capstonepub.com

Copyright © 2024 by Capstone.

All rights reserved. No part of this publication may be reproduced in whole or in part, or stored in a retrieval system, or transmitted in any form or by any means, electronic, mechanical, photocopying, recording, or otherwise, without written permission of the publisher.

Library of Congress Cataloging-in-Publication Data
Names: Maddox, Jake, author. | Deen, Natasha, author. | Malandrino, Maria Lia, illustrator.
Title: Roster rebound / Jake Maddox ; text by Natasha Deen ; illustrated by Maria Lia Malandrino.
Description: North Mankato, Minnesota : Stone Arch Books, an imprint of Capstone, 2023. | Series: Jake Maddox sports stories | Audience: Ages 8 to 11 | Audience: Grades 4–6 | Summary: Since Nina's middle school in her new home in tiny Janesville, Illinois, does not have a girls basketball team, she tries out for the boys team and makes the roster—but the hostility of one the players threatens to disrupt the whole team.
Identifiers: LCCN 2022047855 (print) | LCCN 2022047856 (ebook) | ISBN 9781669033301 (hardcover) | ISBN 9781669033264 (paperback) | ISBN 9781669033271 (pdf) | ISBN 9781669033295 (epub)
Subjects: LCSH: Basketball stories. | Teamwork (Sports)—Juvenile fiction. | Moving, Household—Juvenile fiction. | Middle schools—Juvenile fiction. | Illinois—Juvenile fiction. | CYAC: Basketball—Fiction. | Teamwork (Sports)—Fiction. | Moving, Household—Fiction. | Middle schools—Fiction. | Schools—Fiction. | Illinois—Fiction.
Classification: LCC PZ7.M25643 Rr 2023 (print) | LCC PZ7.M25643 (ebook) | DDC 813.6 [Fic]—dc23/eng/20221014
LC record available at https://lccn.loc.gov/2022047855
LC ebook record available at https://lccn.loc.gov/2022047856

Designer: Sarah Bennett

TABLE OF CONTENTS

CHAPTER ONE
A NEW START 5

CHAPTER TWO
AN UNEXPECTED SURPRISE 11

CHAPTER THREE
SHARKS AT HALF-COURT 17

CHAPTER FOUR
SHARK BITE! 23

CHAPTER FIVE
TRYOUT TIME! 27

CHAPTER SIX
PRACTICE PROBLEMS 34

CHAPTER SEVEN
GAME DAY DISASTER 39

CHAPTER EIGHT
FOUL OUT 47

CHAPTER NINE
FRIENDSHIP PIVOT 52

CHAPTER TEN
GAME ON! 57

CHAPTER ONE

A NEW START

Sunshine glinted off the metal rim of the basketball hoop on Nina Jefferson's driveway. Nina didn't feel the warmth of the sun, though. She told herself she didn't feel warm because she was focusing on perfecting her three-point shot.

But that's not the truth, she thought.

Truthfully, she was using her favorite thing—basketball—to erase the nervousness thrumming through her body. Today was her first day at Willow Heights Middle School.

Her dad's job as a city administrator meant a move from Minnesota to Janesville, Illinois. Even worse than being the new kid was being the new kid in the middle of the school year. Especially in Janesville. It was a tiny town in the middle of nowhere.

Everyone will already have made friends, Nina thought. *Will I spend the rest of the year alone?*

The butterflies fluttered in her stomach. Nina balanced the basketball on her finger and spun it. The lines of the ball blurred and some of the butterflies stopped fluttering.

This was hard to learn, she reminded herself. *If I can do this, I can make friends.*

The sound of the front door opening and closing broke Nina's concentration. *Thump, thump, thump.* The ball bounced and rolled down the driveway. Nina chased after it as her dad came into view. He held up her purple lunch bag.

Dad smiled. "Forget something?"

Nina wanted to smile back, but the anger buzzing inside her made it impossible. This year she'd made captain of her basketball team. The group was amazing—they worked well together on and off the court. Now, she was far from everyone and everything she loved. Nina blinked back the tears.

"Ready to go?" Dad asked.

Nina nodded. Her nervousness made her fingers ice cold. But her anger made her insides red hot.

It's not like I can try out for the team at my new school, she thought.

Three days ago, Nina had sent an email to the school asking about the Willow Heights girls basketball team. The school secretary, Mrs. Lai, had emailed right back. The words in the secretary's reply were still etched in her brain.

Dear Nina,

Thank you so much for your question. The Marmots held girls basketball tryouts two weeks ago. Unfortunately, there weren't enough players interested in trying out, so there is no girls team this year.

Nina bounced the ball on the driveway, harder and harder. She still couldn't believe her new school didn't have a girls team.

"I know this is really difficult," Dad said, gently taking the ball from her. "You're missing your friends and your old team. I am too. But in the long run, this move to Janesville is best for our family. We're closer to Grandma and Grandpa—and there's always next year, right? You can try out for the basketball team then."

Nina took the ball back but didn't respond. She picked up her backpack, climbed inside the car, and slammed the door shut.

As Dad drove to the school, Nina thought about how mad she was at him. Being mad was great. Being mad was *awesome*. If she was mad, she didn't have to think about how nervous she was about the new school and the new kids, or how much she missed her friends.

Nina turned away so Dad couldn't see the tears falling down her cheeks. She swiped them away.

Would this year be her loneliest ever?

CHAPTER TWO

AN UNEXPECTED SURPRISE

Dad stopped at the school drop-off area. "Have a great day, honey!"

"Whatever," Nina said as she stepped out, and then she felt guilty. This job meant fewer hours at work for her dad, which meant more time for them as a family. Plus, Dad was right. They were closer to her grandparents. Being able to visit them every weekend was a bright spot in the gloomy move.

"I'm sorry," Nina told her dad. "I hope you have a great day too."

Dad reached through the open window and gently squeezed her hand. Then he drove away.

When he was out of sight, Nina took a long look at the two-story brick building and then walked inside. As she headed to the office, she noticed a flyer for basketball tryouts.

I missed my chance to try out by two weeks, Nina thought. *It's not fair!*

But her steps slowed when she spotted a few kids crowding around another flyer, chatting excitedly with each other. She went to the pin-up board and peered around the students to get a better look.

Maybe the tryouts are on again. The thought made Nina's heart bounce.

Excitement turned to disappointment when she actually read the flyer. Yes, tryouts were on again. But it was for the Willow Heights Marmots boys team—not the girls.

Nina turned and shuffled to the office. Mrs. Lai greeted Nina as she stepped inside.

"Welcome to Willow Heights!" she said. She handed Nina a schedule and a school map. "If I remember correctly, your email said you were the captain of your basketball team back home, right?"

Nina nodded.

"One of our players had to move away," Mrs. Lai said. "There's a spot for a power forward if you want to try out."

"I saw the flyer." Nina gestured to the hallway. "But it said it was for the boys basketball team."

Mrs. Lai leaned across the counter. "We barely had enough boys for the Marmots' roster to start with. So we've opened up tryouts to everyone."

Nina grinned as the words sunk in. She could try out for the team!

Mrs. Lai phoned Nina's classroom and spoke to the teacher. Then she hung up and turned to Nina.

"A student buddy is coming to collect you," she said. "She'll help you learn the school's layout."

While Nina waited, she daydreamed about making the team.

If I did that, I'd have one thing that's cool in my life, she thought.

The office door opened, and a blonde girl with brown eyes walked inside. She smiled at Nina.

"Hey! I'm Simone Grand," she said. "I'll be your classroom buddy until you get settled!"

Simone's friendliness loosened the nagging tightness in Nina's chest. Maybe she'd found a friend.

"Thanks," she said. "I heard there are basketball tryouts. Can you tell me more?"

"Oh, totally!" Simone leaned forward. "Last year, we came really close to winning the tri-county championships. This year, Cody—he's the captain—is determined to win. The team was set, but *then*—"

"Scoot, you two," said Mrs. Lai as the bell rang. "You'll be late for gym class."

Simone and Nina grinned at each other. Nina followed Simone out the door. Maybe this year wouldn't be a total garbage dump!

CHAPTER THREE

SHARKS AT HALF-COURT

Simone led Nina to the locker room. Two girls were still there. Simone nodded at the red-headed one. "This is Molly." Then she pointed at Nina. "Meet our new classmate, Nina."

Molly smiled at her. The girl next to her stood up and waved. "I'm Laney. Nice to meet you."

Nina waved back. "You too." She still felt worried about being the new kid, but her classmates' friendliness made her feel better.

Nina changed and headed to the gym with the group.

"This is Jack Fuimaono," said Simone, walking up to a black-haired boy. "He's a shooting guard on the basketball team. He'll be super helpful if you want to try out."

Jack's brown eyes lit up. "You want to try out? That's awesome! It's for a power forward."

"I heard. That was my position on my school team back home!" said Nina. She bounced on her toes. Nina couldn't wait until tryouts!

Jack spotted their teacher. "Hey! Coach Popov, check it out! Nina wants to try out for the team." Jack swung back to her. "Our teacher's also the coach."

"That's excellent!" Coach Popov smiled at Nina. "It's great to meet you." He blew his whistle.

"Game on!" Jack said. "It's basketball for our unit!" Then he ran to join the class.

Nina jogged after him.

The warm-up started with stretching and a few laps around the gym.

When the last students finished their lap, Coach Popov said, "Time for a game of sharks and minnows! Ruis Hernandez and Cody Jones, you're up! You will be the sharks. Take your position on the half-court line. The rest of the class are minnows. Grab a basketball and head to the baseline."

Simone ran to the bag of basketballs and handed them out. Then she joined Nina.

"The minnows will dribble from one end of the gym to the other," said Coach Popov. "The sharks will try to knock the basketball out of their hands. If that happens, the minnow joins the sharks."

"Oh brother, forget it," Simone muttered to Nina. "Ruis and Cody are the best players on the team. We'll all be sharks soon!"

Nina grinned at the challenge. *I'm amazing at dribbling,* she thought.

Coach Popov blew his whistle. The minnows dribbled toward the other end of the gym. Ruis ran to Nina, but she was ready for him. As Ruis tried to slap away the ball, she pivoted and kept it away. The cheers and howls as minnows lost their balls to sharks followed her as she raced down the court.

Suddenly, Nina heard the hard pounding of feet behind her. Cody appeared beside her, trying to get the ball away. Nina deked left and then right. When Cody blocked her path, she bounced the ball through his legs and then dribbled to the finish line.

Simone and Jack ran over and gave her high fives.

"Nice job, new kid!" Ruis held up his hand.

"My name is Nina." She grinned and gave him a high five.

Coach Popov blew his whistle. "Time for a change-up! Cody, stay on as a shark," he said. "Ruis, you're a minnow. Nina, you're a shark!" Coach grinned at her and Cody. "But there's an extra challenge for the two of you."

Cody and Nina looked at each other. What did Coach Popov have in store?

"This time," said Coach Popov, "you and Cody will also dribble a ball."

Cody's eyes widened. "Why?" he asked. "That makes it so much harder!"

Coach Popov laughed. "Exactly. Let's see what the two of you've got!"

Everyone jogged to their positions. Coach Popov blew his whistle. Nina was determined to win again. She quickly turned several minnows into sharks.

As the game went on, the remaining players turned out to be great at keep-away. Then an idea sparked in Nina's head.

"Cody, get alongside me!" she said.

Cody did, and Nina nodded toward Molly.

"Now, you go on one side of Molly, and I'll take the other," she said.

Cody nodded.

Once they were parallel, Nina shouted, "Close in!" They moved closer to Molly, and Cody batted the ball down the court.

"Next one," Cody said. "Simone."

They dribbled to Simone and quickly got the ball away.

"Is that allowed?" Simone asked, laughing and trying to catch her breath.

"I didn't say anything about having to work alone," said Coach Popov. He blew his whistle. "Great strategy, Nina!"

Nina blushed with pleasure. Maybe this school wouldn't be so bad after all. There was a spot in her heart that had been hurting since the move. Right now, it didn't hurt so much.

"Great teamwork!" Nina said and held up her hand for a high five from Cody.

He scowled at her instead. "I was just doing what I needed to do to win. We're not a team."

Cody stalked off, and Nina stared after him in shock. Her friends back home would never have been so mean to anyone. What had she done to deserve that?

CHAPTER FIVE

TRYOUT TIME!

"Don't worry about him," Simone said, coming up to Nina. "He's been growly ever since Liam moved last week."

"Liam?" asked Nina.

"They were best friends," said Simone, fixing her ponytail. "But Liam had to move for his mom's work."

Hmm, thought Nina, *I definitely know what that feels like.*

"I was thinking of trying out for the team," Nina said, "but now I'm not so sure. I don't want to spend the whole season with Cody glaring at me."

"He'll get over it," said Simone. "And you should try out! I'll come and cheer you on!"

* * *

At lunchtime on Friday, Nina headed to the gym. She sat on the bench, jiggling her legs. Molly and Laney sat beside her. Like them, she hoped to be the Marmots' newest power forward.

Nina looked to the bleachers. Simone was on the sidelines. She waved and cheered.

Coach Popov blew his whistle. "Let's go, everyone!"

He took them through a warm-up with laps. Next up were shooting drills. Nina missed a few of the rebound shots but nailed the three-pointers.

"Okay, folks," said Coach Popov. "It's scrimmage time."

Nina partnered with Molly and Laney for a three-on-three. On the other team were Cody, Jack, and Ruis.

Molly and Cody faced each other at the half-court line. Nina and Laney took their places behind Molly. Jack and Ruis stood behind Cody.

Coach Popov stepped in between Molly and Cody. He blew his whistle and then tossed the ball into the air.

Both players leaped, and Cody swatted the jump ball to Ruis. As he dribbled toward the wing, Nina caught up to him. When Ruis tried to pass the ball back to Cody, Nina jumped up and caught it!

Spinning on her heel, Nina spotted Molly and passed to her. Molly dribbled the ball to the free-throw line and passed to Laney.

As Nina raced to an open position, Laney tossed her the ball. Nina caught it, took a shot, and—*SWISH*—it went in.

"Nothing but net!" cried Nina.

Cody caught the ball, ran toward the sidelines, and threw it to Jack. He dribbled to his net and took a shot from the three-point line. The ball bounced off the rim.

Nina snatched the rebound and tossed the ball to Laney. As Laney dribbled down the lane, Nina raced alongside. Jack matched her stride for stride.

"Pass to me!" Nina cried.

Cody blocked Laney and waved his arms. But Laney leaned to one side and squeaked a bounce pass to Nina.

As Jack closed in to guard, Nina dribbled once and then faked a pass back to Laney. While Jack moved to block the pass, Nina took the jump shot.

The ball arced high in the air and sailed through the hoop. *SWISH!* Three points for her team!

By the end of the tryout, Nina was totally exhausted but happy.

Even if I don't make the team, it was super cool to be part of a group, she thought.

"Thanks, everyone. I have a tough decision to make," said Coach Popov. "But I'll post the name of the new team member on my office door by the end of the day."

The rest of the afternoon felt like a slow-motion blur for Nina. All she wanted was to get to Coach's office.

As soon as the bell rang, Simone looked at Nina. "Let's go!"

They zipped down the hall. When they reached the coach's office, Nina spotted a folded piece of paper taped to the door. She unfolded it and read the name printed inside.

NINA JEFFERSON

She'd made the team!

"You did it!" Simone whooped, hugging Nina. "You're the new power forward!"

Nina danced in celebration. This year was looking up!

Just then, she spotted Cody walking by. He glared at her and kept walking. Nina's delight changed to worry. How would she survive the season with a teammate who didn't want her to be part of the team?

CHAPTER SIX

PRACTICE PROBLEMS

Nina used the weekend to practice at home. When Tuesday rolled around, and it was time for her first practice with the team, her nerves were tight. If Cody wasn't happy to have her as part of the team, what would the other players' reactions be? She took a breath and left the locker room.

As soon as she walked into the gym, the team erupted into cheers. Nina breathed out a sigh of relief.

At least they're happy to have me on the team, she thought.

After everyone had introduced themselves, Coach Popov started their warm-up.

The familiarity of ball-handling drills and dribbling exercises felt comfortable. If it was up to her, she'd spend all day in the gym. Well, she'd change one thing. Cody. No matter what she did, he criticized her.

When they were practicing their shooting, he complained, "You're letting the ball go too quickly on the layup. You'll never get baskets that way."

Nina reminded herself that he was having a rough time with his friend moving, and she stayed quiet.

It was hard to do, though. Especially when they were partnered for two-on-two drills. After the last play, he'd glared at her and said, "You should have gotten to the key faster."

By the end of practice, Nina was done with his bad mood and sharp words.

"I'm a good player," she told Cody. "You need to back off."

"You're good," he said, "But you're not great. You shouldn't have made the team."

"I was the captain on my last team!" she said. "Is it because I'm a girl?"

Cody snorted. "I don't care about you being a girl," he said. "I care about winning. When Liam was here, we were a shoo-in for the championships. Now, who knows?" He walked away, stopped, and turned. "Wait," he said. "I know. With you on the team, we're never going to win."

Nina took a breath to yell at him. Then she felt Jack's hand on her shoulder.

"It's not worth it," Jack said. "You're a great player and the rest of us are glad to have you on the team. I'll talk to him."

Jack's words made Nina feel a little better, but not a lot. Cody's meanness was taking the fun out of making the team. Every time he talked to her, she thought about how her former team had always worked hard to make each other feel like they belonged.

Nina sat on the bench and sipped her water. The ache in her heart gave way to a fire growing in her belly.

If Cody doesn't think I'm great, she thought, *he's about to get a big surprise. I'll show him how wrong he is at our first game.*

CHAPTER SEVEN

GAME DAY DISASTER

A week and a half later, it was Nina's first game with the Marmots. They were taking on the Riverbend Ravens. She was nervous but determined to show her skills.

In the locker room, Nina adjusted her jersey and kicked out the nervousness in her legs. She was more anxious about Cody than about the game. Even though the other players had become her friends, it felt like Cody was always waiting for her to make a mistake.

Nina jogged from the locker room to the gym. Just as she got to the bench, the Ravens arrived. Both teams began their warm-ups.

"They're a solid team," Jack said. "But we beat them last time." He nudged her. "With you on the team, we'll beat them again."

Nina grinned. "My team and I used to go for burgers after the game. Maybe we can do that today too?"

"For sure!" Jack said. Then he nodded at a Ravens player with the number eighteen on his shirt. "That's Douglas. He's the one to watch. He could carry his team by himself!"

Cody, who was stretching near them, straightened. "Forget about your burgers," he said. "We need to win the game first."

Nina rolled her eyes and went to a different spot to finish warming up. She looked up and saw her dad sitting with Simone. They waved at her.

A few minutes later, the referee blew the whistle and tossed the jump ball. It was game on!

Cody caught the ball and dribbled it toward the lane. He deked around a Ravens player and passed to Ruis. Nina ran alongside.

"I'm open!" She called.

Ruis passed to her.

Nina ran to the lane and bounce-passed to Cody. He dribbled a few steps and then took a shot. The ball went in! The Marmots were the first to have points on the board!

A tall Ravens player—wearing number twenty-four—stepped out of bounds to make the inbound pass. He quickly launched the ball to his teammate, number eighteen.

That's Douglas, Nina thought, remembering what Jack had said. She chased after Douglas, but he dribbled around her and took a shot. It went in.

"It's just one basket," Nina called out as Cody caught the ball. "We've got this!"

Cody went to the sidelines and then tossed the ball to Jack. He dribbled to the Marmots' home key.

But Douglas was as good as Jack had warned. As Jack pivoted, looking for his teammates, Douglas slapped the ball. It bounced to his teammate, who raced toward their net.

Cody gave chase, but the Ravens player took a shot. When the ball bounced off the rim, Cody jumped for it. But the Ravens player grabbed the rebound and banked a shot off the backboard. This time, the ball went in.

By halftime, the Ravens were ahead 22–12. Nina sat on the bench, catching her breath.

"You weren't kidding about Douglas," she said to Jack.

Jack nodded. "He's gotten better since our last game." He took a swig of his water. "We can still win, though!"

To start the second half, the referee handed the ball to a Ravens player on the sidelines. When the ref blew his whistle, the Ravens tossed the ball inbounds. One of his teammates caught the pass, and the teams fell into their formations.

All through the second half, Nina did her best. But Cody was a constant distraction.

When the Ravens surrounded her and she tried to pass to Jack, Cody yelled, "Don't pass! Dribble down the court."

But when Nina tried her best to follow his instructions, a Ravens player slapped the ball away from her and took control.

As the game stretched on, Nina's thoughts raced. *Cody's making me question myself—but I know I'm good at this!*

"Stop daydreaming!" Cody yelled on cue. "Cover Douglas!"

Nina jumped into action, chased him down, and intercepted a pass. She dribbled back to her side and then took her shot at the basket. It missed.

Douglas snagged the rebound and raced to his basket. As Nina tried to block his shot, she accidentally tripped him.

The referee blew his whistle.

"Great. You fouled him." Cody scowled at Nina. "He gets two free throws because of you."

Nina swallowed her angry reply. Cody was getting in her head and causing her to make silly mistakes.

The players lined up and Douglas took his first shot.

Nina groaned as it went in. She groaned again when Douglas's second shot went in too.

The rest of the game didn't go much better. In the end, the Marmots lost 43–35.

"This is your fault!" Cody stalked toward her. His face was red. "We could've won the game if you were a better player!"

His words stung. Nina already felt horrible about the loss and was convinced that she'd let down the team. She headed to the locker room, her steps slow and weary.

Maybe I should just quit, she thought. *Basketball doesn't feel like my happy place anymore.*

CHAPTER EIGHT

FOUL OUT

That night, Nina talked to her dad while they were making dinner.

"I understand," he said. "Being around someone who makes every moment difficult isn't easy." He fluffed the rice in the pot. "Here's my question. If you quit, will you be happy with the decision? Or will you regret allowing Cody to push you away from something you love?"

"I don't know," she said.

"Take your time and think about the answer," said Dad. "Whatever choice you make, I'll support you."

The next morning, Nina woke up knowing her choice. She wasn't going to let Cody decide for her. Nina loved basketball, and she knew she was good at it. Great at it, in fact! No one could have a perfect game all the time. Sure, she'd missed a couple of shots, but she'd done her best, and that's what mattered.

* * *

On Tuesday, Nina headed into practice determined to ignore Cody. The rest of the team liked her, and she liked them. As she entered the gym, she spotted Simone.

"Is it okay if I watch?" Simone asked. "Maybe we can grab ice cream after?"

"That would be awesome," said Nina. She walked onto the court and focused on Jack and Ruis.

We do a great job together, she thought. *Who cares if Cody doesn't want to be my friend?*

But as soon as practice started, Cody started in on Nina once again.

"Your layups don't have any power," he said. "We'll never win if you don't practice harder."

"Stop it, Cody!" Nina said. "And back off! I was the captain of my team back home. We won championships because we worked together to help each player be the best they could be. Do you think yelling at me is helpful? How about giving me some tips instead?"

Before he could answer, Ruis stepped forward. "She's right," he said. "You haven't been a great teammate to Nina."

Jack put his hand on Cody's shoulder. "It's not like you to act like this. We know you're upset because Liam left, but—"

Cody jerked away from Jack and rounded on Nina. "Are you happy now? You've turned the team against me. Maybe I should just quit and let you take over as captain. I bet that's what you wanted all along." Cody stormed off.

Nina started to follow him, but Ruis pulled her back.

"Let him have a minute," Ruis said. "He'll realize he's being unfair."

Maybe, but if Cody quits, the team suffers. Nina's heart sank at the thought. They'd need to have another round of tryouts.

When practice was over, Simone came up to Nina. "I'm so sorry—Cody shouldn't have said any of that."

Nina shrugged. She was too afraid she'd start crying if she tried to talk.

"How about that ice cream?" said Simone. "Double scoop. My treat."

Nina changed in the locker room. Then she and Simone headed out.

"I feel terrible," Nina told her friend as they walked to the ice cream shop. "I know I did the right thing in standing up for myself, but did it just cost the team the season?"

CHAPTER NINE
FRIENDSHIP PIVOT

On Friday, Nina headed to the gym for their game against the Cottondale Coyotes. The tightness in her chest eased when she saw Cody warming up. At least he hadn't quit.

And thank goodness! From what Jack and Ruis had told her, they'd need to bring their A game if they were going to win.

Nina watched Cody and debated going over to talk to him. Then she remembered Ruis's advice and decided to leave him alone.

Nina found a spot far away from Cody and started stretching. But he saw her and slowly walked over.

Nina braced herself for another round of harsh words.

"I'm sorry," he said.

Nina blinked in surprise. This wasn't what she had expected.

"Ruis, you—all of you were right about me being mean. It's just—" Cody dropped his gaze. "Liam left, and then suddenly you were here. You took his spot, and everyone was so great to you . . . and it felt like no one was remembering him."

Cody shuffled his feet and ran his fingers through his hair. Then he looked at her.

"And it felt like if I was your friend right away, somehow it meant that Liam and I weren't best friends," he said. "That probably doesn't make any sense—"

"It totally makes sense," Nina said. "I'm having a hard time too. I really miss my friends back home. Sometimes it feels like when I'm having fun here I'm not being loyal to my old team."

"I'm really sorry," Cody told her. "I should have treated you better." He ducked his head. "I should have seen it from your point of view, being the new kid in school. I'd hate it if anyone was mean to Liam the way I've been to you."

"I can't take Liam's place." Nina put her hand on Cody's shoulder. "And I shouldn't. You were best friends. I can be another friend though." She grinned and bumped his shoulder. "I can also ignore you if that would make you feel better."

Cody laughed. "No, it wouldn't. I want to be friends. And I promise, no more yelling at you to change your plays during the game."

Nina put out her hand. "Deal!"

Cody shook it. "Now, let's go get those Coyotes!" He ran to the huddle.

Nina looked for Simone and her dad in the stands. When she saw them, she gave them a thumbs-up. Then she ran to join her team.

Cody had it right. It was time to get those Coyotes!

CHAPTER TEN

GAME ON!

In preparation for the jump ball, Nina stood opposite one of the Coyotes players.

He grinned. "Good luck, but we're going to win!"

Nina grinned back. "Go ahead and try!"

The referee blew her whistle and tossed the ball between them. Nina jumped and tipped the ball to Ruis. As Ruis dribbled toward the basket, Cody set a screen on a Coyotes defender and then pivoted toward the net. Ruis passed him the ball and Cody jumped to take the shot.

But the Coyotes were ready for them. Just as Cody released the ball, one of the Coyotes defenders smacked it away. Another Coyote snatched the ball, dribbled down the court, and lobbed it. His teammate caught the ball and easily scored with a layup.

Down early, the Marmots did their best to rally as the first half unfolded. But nearly every play was blocked by the Coyotes. By halftime, the Marmots were down by ten points, 17–27.

Nina scanned her teammates' faces. She saw a lot of furrowed brows. They looked as frustrated as she felt.

Cody caught her gaze. "Sometimes it's just a bad game, no matter how hard you try. You're doing great."

Nina smiled. "Thanks."

"Okay, team, throw ideas at me," their coach said, crouching in front of the bench.

As the team gathered around to discuss the plays, Cody turned to Nina.

"I know I said I wouldn't tell you to change how you're playing," he said, "but maybe it's time to shake things up."

"I'm up for it," said Nina.

Cody leaned into the group. "Okay, this is what we're going to do . . ."

* * *

At the start of the second half, the Marmots took to the court. Nina went to the sidelines. The referee blew his whistle and bounce-passed her the ball. She tossed the ball inbounds to Jack. He dribbled down the lane and tossed it back to her, but a Coyotes player intercepted it.

It was time to put Cody's plan into action—apply constant pressure to their opponent. As the opposing players set their screens, Cody and Jack raced for the basket.

The Coyotes player took the shot and Jack caught it on the rebound. He zipped the ball to Cody, who raced to their basket and took the shot. It went in! The Marmots were catching up!

By the middle of the fourth quarter, the strategy had paid off. The teams were tied. One of the Coyotes took possession and launched the ball down court. As they neared the basket, one of the players fired off a quick shot. It bounced off the backboard and Jack caught it.

He headed for the Marmots' hoop and passed to Cody, who took the shot. It missed. Cody grabbed the rebound, but missed his second shot too.

As the plays continued, Nina watched the clock. Time was counting down, but neither team could break the tie. When there was only twenty seconds left on the clock, she knew this was their final chance.

Jack took a shot, but it was an air ball. A Coyotes player caught it. He dribbled the ball down the court.

Nina chased him down and got in front of him. As he tried to get around her, she knocked the ball out of his hand.

Ruis grabbed the loose ball and threw it back to her. Spinning in the opposite direction, she headed over the half-court line and kept her eye out for one of her teammates.

"Nina!" she heard Cody yell. "Pass it to Ruis!"

She did, and then she raced down the lane. Ruis dribbled the ball a couple times and sent it back to Cody, who took the shot. The ball bounced off the rim!

Nina got under the basket and caught the rebound. She dodged around a Coyotes player and then took a shot.

The basketball sailed through the net just as the buzzer sounded. The Marmots won the game!

Nina held up her hand for a high five. This time, Cody was there to high-five her back.

"Great teamwork, Nina!" He grinned. "Time for burgers!"

"Awesome!" said Nina.

They headed off to join the rest of the team.

AUTHOR BIO

photo by Richard Jervis

Natasha Deen loves stories—scary ones, exciting ones, and especially funny ones! She lives in Edmonton, Alberta, Canada, with her family, where she spends a lot of time trying to convince her pets that she's the boss of the house.

ILLUSTRATOR BIO

photo by M. L. Malandrino

Maria Lia Malandrino is an illustrator based in Torino, Italy. She grew up reading fantasy books and comics, knowing that fictional universes are often just as real and powerful as our own world. In her free time, Maria likes playing strategy and role-playing games or being outdoors—rowing on the river that flows through her hometown or hiking with her young family and dog

GLOSSARY

administrator (ad-MIN-uh-stray-tur)—a person who leads a business or organization

deke (DEEK)—to pretend to go one way, then go in the other direction; it is a move used to trick opposing players

dribble (DRIB-uhl)—to continuously bounce a basketball with one hand; dribbling is the only way a player can move the ball around the court while maintaining possession

intercept (in-tur-SEPT)—to catch a pass made by an opposing player

lane (LAYN)—the area on a basketball court underneath the basket and bounded by the end line and the foul line

pressure (PRESH-ur)—a strong influence or force applied to an opposing player or team

rally (RAL-ee)—to make a comeback

rebound (REE-bound)—to catch the basketball after a shot has been missed

screen (SKREEN)—a move by an offensive player to block a defensive player in order to free up a teammate to pass, shoot, get open, or drive to the basket

shoo-in (SHOO-in)—someone or something that is certain to succeed

DISCUSSION QUESTIONS

1. On her first day at her new school, Nina uses basketball to help calm her nerves. When you feel nervous, what are some things you do to find your calm?

2. Willow Heights is too small to have separate boys and girls teams. How do you feel about girls playing on boys teams and vice versa?

3. Nina's teammates step in when Cody is mean to her. Has there ever been a time you helped someone who was being bullied? What did you do?

WRITING PROMPTS

1. When Coach Popov pairs up Nina and Cody for a round of sharks and minnows, he adds the extra challenge of having them dribble a basketball. Write a paragraph about why you think he did this.

2. Nina has to decide whether she wants to keep playing basketball or if Cody's behavior is too much to handle. Have you experienced something similar? Write about that memory.

3. Nina lucks out at her new school because the Marmots are having tryouts. Write a paragraph about how Nina might have made friends if the tryouts hadn't happened.

BASKETBALL LINGO

Basketball has unique game-play lingo. Here are some terms to help you enjoy the sport:

air ball: a shot at the basket in which the ball doesn't touch the backboard, net, or rim

assist: a pass to a teammate who then shoots and scores

fast break: a quick offensive drive to the basket, attempting to beat the defense down the court

free throw: also known as a foul shot, free throws are awarded after a player is fouled by someone on the opposing team; each free throw is worth one point

jump ball: a method of putting a basketball into play; the referee throws the basketball into the air between two opposing players, who jump up and attempt to direct the ball to a teammate

jump shot: a shot made while jumping and releasing the ball at the peak of the jump

layup: a two-point shot made from very close to the basket, usually by bouncing the ball off the backboard

rim: the metal circle on a basketball hoop

starting five: the group of players who are on the court at the beginning and most of the game

three-pointer: a successful shot from outside the designated arc of the three-point line on a basketball court

THE FUN DOESN'T STOP HERE!

DISCOVER MORE JAKE MADDOX BOOKS AT:

capstonepub.com

AND KEEP THE SPORTS ACTION GOING!